ELMER
AND SNAKE

David McKee

Andersen Press
London

Elmer, the patchwork elephant, was thinking.
He was thinking that it was a nice day for doing nothing.
Nearby were two other elephants. "Look," whispered one.
"Elmer is thinking up a trick to play on us. Let's play a trick
on him instead."

"What shall we do?" asked the other elephant.

"I don't know. I can never think of tricks,"
said the first. "But Snake will know."

Off they went to see Snake.

"Hello, Snake," they said. "We want to play a trick on Elmer. What can we do?"

Snake thought, then chuckled. "Tell him he's looking pale. Get him to lie down and rest."

"He'll see that *that's* not true," said one of the elephants.

Snake sniggered. "If it's repeated often enough he'll believe it. You'll see."

The elephants weren't convinced – but they agreed
to try Snake's idea because they didn't have any other.
On the way home they asked other animals to help
them fool Elmer.

Meanwhile, Snake sneaked off and told Elmer
the idea. "Do as they say, Elmer, and lie down where you
usually do," he said. "I'll bring some white mud from the
pool and rub you with it. It will make you look pale.
They want to trick you, but we'll trick them."

"All right, Snake," said Elmer. "I feel like lying down
and doing nothing. I'll have a walk first."

Soon after, Elmer met Leopard who said,
"Are you feeling all right, Elmer? You look pale."
"Do I?" said Elmer. "Oh dear!"
Then every animal that Elmer met said,
"Are you feeling all right, Elmer? You look pale."
And Elmer said, "Do I? Oh dear!"

While Elmer returned to the other elephants,
Snake was busy dragging a very large leaf
towards Elmer's favourite lying-down place.
On the leaf was a pile of white mud.

"Here comes Elmer," the elephants whispered to each other.
Then out loud they said, "Are you feeling all right, Elmer?
You look pale. You should lie down and rest."
Elmer just nodded and went to his usual place.
"It's working," chuckled the elephants.

Snake was ready and, using a smaller leaf,
covered Elmer with a thin coat of mud.
Elmer giggled.

"Stop it, they'll notice," said Snake, then finished
and hid. Elmer was left with his colours looking
paler under the thin coat of mud.

"I'll go and peep at Elmer," said an elephant.

Elmer was asleep. Being covered with mud is relaxing, especially when you feel like doing nothing.

The elephant returned to the others. "He's very quiet," he said. "And he really does look pale."

The elephants laughed. One said, "Snake said that if we told Elmer often enough he'd believe it. Now you're believing it, too. Go and look again."

While they were talking, Snake gently covered Elmer with more mud. Elmer slept on.

The elephant found Elmer paler than ever and
hurried away to get the others. Snake covered Elmer
yet again then hid as the elephants arrived.

"He's getting paler all the time," said the first
elephant. "What shall we do?"

"We'll have to ask Snake," said another.
Snake heard and hurried home.

When the elephants arrived, Snake was waiting.
He acted surprised. "Believing you are ill can make you ill,"
he said. "The way to cure Elmer is to tickle him."
At first the elephants were shocked but Snake
convinced them and they hurried away to try the cure.

Elmer woke feeling strange. The mud had dried, making a stiff cover all over him.

At the same time, the elephants tiptoed up and started to tickle him. Elmer laughed and jumped up, bursting out of his mud shell like a chick breaking out of an egg. His colours showed as normal.

"Hurrah!" shouted the elephants. "It worked. Snake was right."

Elmer laughed. "Snake? He's a crafty one!
You thought you were tricking me, I thought I was tricking
you, and Snake tricked all of us. It's Snake we should tickle."
But Snake, being sensible, had gone on holiday.
So the elephants tickled each other and anyone else that was
around, until the jungle rocked with the sound of laughter.